Play Time

Written by Roger Paré
with Bertrand Gauthier
and illustrated by Roger Paré

English adaptation by David Homel

Annick Press Ltd.
Toronto, Ontario

Second Printing, August 1990

Annick Press gratefully acknowledges
the support of The Canada Council

Canadian Cataloguing in Publication Data

Paré, Roger, 1929-
   (Plaisirs d'aimer. English)
   Play time

Translation of: Plaisirs d'aimer.
ISBN 1-55037-087-1 (bound) ISBN 1-55037-086-3 (pbk.)

I. Gauthier, Bertrand, 1945-   . II. Homel, David.
III. Title. IV. Title: Plaisirs d'aimer. English.

PS8581.A697P5213 1990   jC843′.54   C89-095161-6
PZ7.P375P1 1990

Originally published by
La Courte Echelle, Montreal, Quebec

Distributed in Canada and the USA by:
Firefly Books Ltd.
250 Sparks Avenue
Willowdale, Ontario, M2H 2S4

 This book is printed on acid free paper

Printed and bound in Canada by
D.W. Friesen & Sons, Ltd.

For Justine

When the monkey family
strolls down the street,
they dance and sing
and stomp their feet.

It's party-time
for cat and mice.
Would you like some cheese
or strawberry ice?

I'll do your portrait
if you just sit still.
But my nose will itch,
I know it will!

The curtain's up,
let the show begin,
starring Sir Lion
and Miss Leopard Skin.

Listen to the music
floating down the hall.
It's the rhino's band
getting ready for the ball.

This monster mama
is having loads of fun,
laughing and giggling
and tickling her son.

A fox ballgame
on a sunny day.
Who's going to win?
It's hard to say.

A big fat bear
with a big fat tummy,
eating big fat apples,
are they ever yummy!

A moonlit kiss
on a furry cheek,
while the hoot-owls call
and the field mice squeak.

I love reading
with Grandma Mary,
her stories are funny
and sometimes scary.

Other Annick Press books by Roger Paré:

A FRIEND LIKE YOU

SUMMER DAYS

CIRCUS DAYS